Who's Sick Today?

by Lynne Cherry

VOYAGER BOOKS   HARCOURT BRACE & COMPANY   San Diego   New York   London

This book is dedicated to Nancy and David Dougherty, Nancy Drye
and Bob Thomas, Gloria and Walt Hallagan, Ellen Calmus,
Jim Huffman and the house on Rosedale Road.

Requests for permission to make copies of any part of the work should
be mailed to: Permissions Department, Harcourt Brace & Company,
6277 Sea Harbor Drive, Orlando, Florida 32887-6777.

Previously published by E. P. Dutton, a division of NAL Penguin Inc.

First Voyager Books edition 1998
Voyager Books is a registered trademark of Harcourt Brace & Company.

Library of Congress Cataloging-in-Publication Data
Cherry, Lynne.
Who's sick today?/by Lynne Cherry.
p.   cm.
"Voyager Books."
Summary: Rhyming text and illustrations introduce a variety of
animals with different ailments.
ISBN 0-15-201886-7
[1. Sick–Fiction.   2. Animals–Fiction.   3. Stories in rhyme.]   I. Title.
PZ8.3.C427Wh 1998
[E]–dc21   97-32654

A C E F D B

Printed in Hong Kong

Printed by South China Printing Company, Hong Kong
Production supervision by Stanley Redfern and Jane Van Gelder

Who's sick today?

Beavers with fevers,

a snake with an ache,

a small red fox with chicken pox.

Who's at the doctor today?

A whale on a scale,

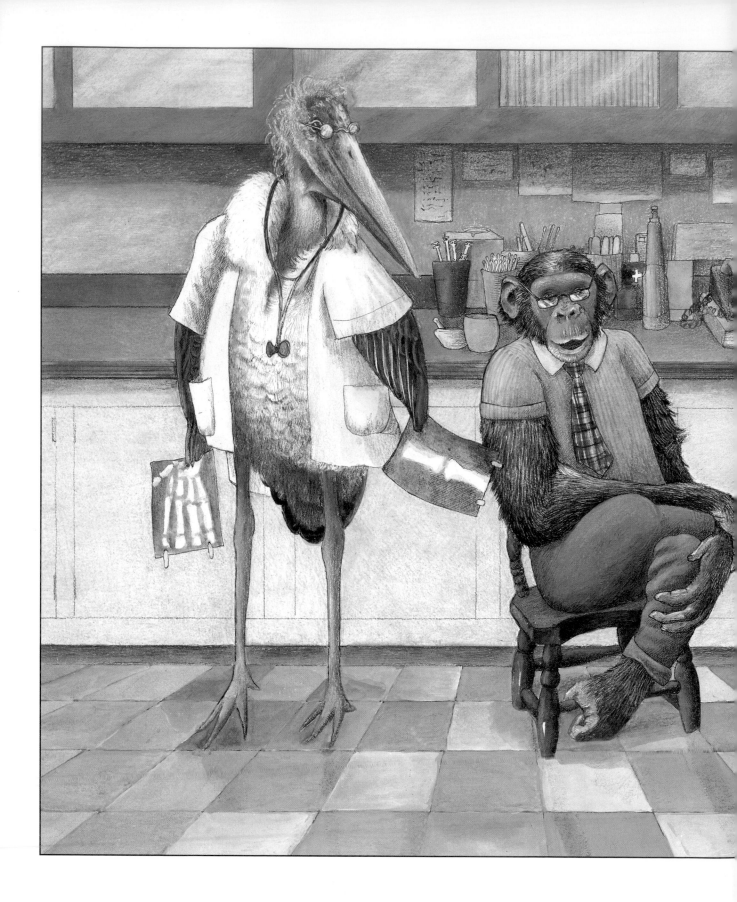

a chimp with a limp,

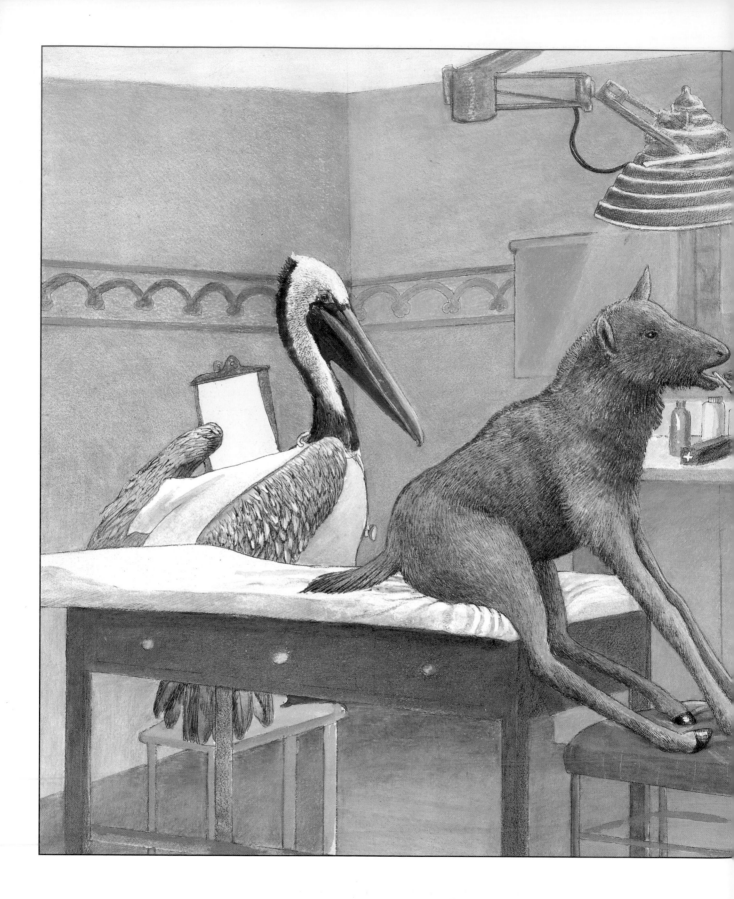

a gnu with the flu.

Who's in the hospital today?

Llamas in pajamas,

young stoats with sore throats,

cranes with pains,

possums with blossoms,

and baboons with balloons.

Who's all better today?
A porcupine who's feeling fine!